comix

HOT AIR

Anthony Masters

Illustrated by Mike Perkins

Read about our trip of terror in a runaway hot air balloon!

With many thanks to Andy Elson
for his advice about hot air balloons.

comix

First paperback edition 2002
First published 2002 in hardback by
A & C Black (Publishers) Ltd
37 Soho Square, London, W1D 3QZ

ISBN 0-7136-5964-5

A CIP catalogue for this book is available from the
British Library.

Printed and bound in Spain by G. Z. Printek, Bilbao

CHAPTER ONE

Steve watched his uncle Harry get out of the basket. He was about to unhitch the balloon's mooring rope.

Okay, let's go for lift off!

He grinned at Steve.

You got that pet rat of yours safe?

You bet, Buster's fine.

There was a muffled squeaking from his pocket.

4

Suddenly a funny look came over Uncle Harry's face and his hand went to his chest. Then he fell to the ground, gasping for breath.

Steve gazed down at him in horror. So did his cousins, Will and Joe. Harry was their father and they could see he was ill.

Buster squeaked in alarm and Steve tickled his back to comfort him.

But he was only trying to keep his cousins calm.
There was everything to worry about.

Uncle Harry had dropped the mooring rope and the balloon was slowly floating up into the grey sky.

He was right. The balloon was far too high to jump from. But this was the boys' first flight and none of them had any idea how to bring it down.

Above them the burner roared with a red flame.

That's what keeps
the balloon going up.
If someone shuts off
the burner,
surely the balloon
should come down.
But how do you shut
off the burner?

Steve's throat was so dry he could hardly speak.

Will and Joe looked at him uneasily.

CHAPTER TWO

Steve gazed up at the red flame. He hadn't a clue.

His voice broke. None of the boys wanted to show how scared they were.

Steve looked down. They must be hundreds of feet above the ground already and Uncle Harry was still lying in the field. There was no one else around.

14

Steve gazed up at the tear-shaped red and blue balloon. A wind was getting up, and there were dark storm clouds on the horizon.

Steve had been looking forward to his first trip in a hot air balloon. Today he was eleven years old and this was his birthday treat. Some treat, he thought. The balloon was moving fast now.

Will and Joe were twins, a year younger than Steve. They looked helpless. Somehow Steve knew he had to take the decisions. He examined the burner and saw a brass toggle.

Steve looked over the side of the basket. The ground was much further away and they were heading for the cliffs. Beyond the cliffs was the sea. The wind was still rising. So was the balloon.

Steve could see breakers hitting the shingle beach and, further out, white wave crests rolling along. There was a lot of spray. He hesitated.

Then, with sudden decision, he pulled at the toggle and the burner shut down.

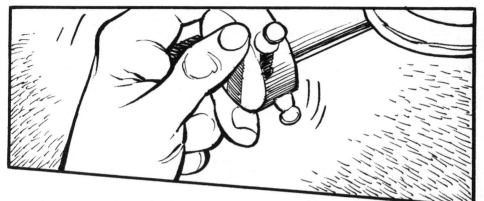

There was no more roaring. No more flames. Then the balloon began to drift down towards the cliffs. Buster squeaked and struggled.

We're coming down too fast.

CHAPTER THREE

As the balloon lost height, Steve suddenly saw the pylons in the valley just below the cliffs.

Steve gazed up at the burner and pulled the rod back into its original position.

Nothing happened and the balloon continued to drift down. Then suddenly the burner fired and the bright red flame flared. The balloon began to rise again, but Steve was sure he'd left it too late to clear the pylons. They loomed up at them like a giant's steel fingers.

Then, just as they were bracing themselves for the collision, the balloon suddenly soared, clearing the cables by a few inches.

22

The basket rocked crazily. But the wind was too strong and they kept heading towards the sea.

Will grabbed his mobile.

Will punched the buttons, his fingers trembling. Suddenly the phone went dead — no signal.

Steve hesitated. The beach wasn't very wide. He grabbed the rod and shut down the burner. Slowly the balloon began to drift down again.

At first Steve thought they might just make the beach. But the wind was still too strong.

Then Steve saw the flashing lights of a police car and ambulance speeding down the coast road.

Look! Your dad must have recovered. He's called the rescue services.

What can they do? We're drifting out to sea.

Will was panicking badly and Steve tried to calm him.

They'll launch the lifeboat.

Steve wanted to reassure the twins, but he was beginning to feel sick himself.

And the air-sea rescue. Like calling out a helicopter.

The balloon was clear of the beach now and they were out over the sea, the breaking swell glistening with spray.

If we're going to hit the waves, thought Steve, will the balloon and the basket float? Or will they sink and drag us down with them?

CHAPTER FOUR

Steve was just about to grab the rod again.

He glanced back to see the police car and ambulance had driven up on the cliff-top. They were flashing their headlights at the drifting balloon. Steve felt a bit more reassured.

The twins stared silently back at him.

Steve began to worry about Buster who was still squirming about in his pocket and squeaking miserably. He'd been his pet for a year now and they did everything together. How was he going to keep Buster safe?

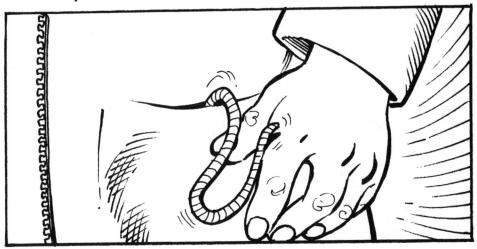

Then he had an idea. Lying in the basket was Steve's sandwich box.

Steve pulled out the struggling white rat and dumped him in the box. Then he took out his penknife and punched six small holes in the lid. Steve reckoned that this way Buster would be able to breathe but hopefully not too much water could get in.

Fumbling with the strings of his jacket, Steve managed to strap the sandwich box inside the hood at the back of his neck.

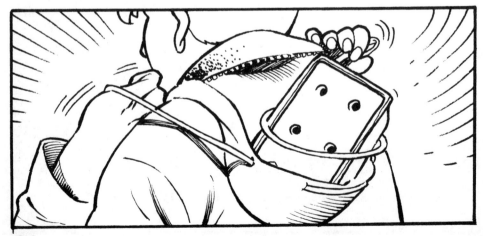

When he looked down again he saw the balloon was much nearer to the heaving sea. The waves lashed and the wind howled.

Then Will remembered something important.

Steve nodded, thinking of the warm water of the indoor swimming pool.

Cold spray from a huge rolling wave then hit him in the face. He shivered miserably.

Joe and Will shook their heads.

CHAPTER FIVE

Steve reckoned the balloon was only around twenty feet above the waves.

Steve's stomach was churning like the waves as he checked the horizon. Where was the stupid lifeboat? There was a clap of thunder and then the rain came down, hard and strong, lashing the waves.

Steve had another unsettling thought.

Steve's heart pounded. How was he going to save Will and Joe — as well as Buster? The basket was skimming the surface now and they were already soaked by spray.

But then Steve realised Uncle Harry had intended to fly inland.

The basket hit the waves first and turned on its side, throwing them into the sea. Then the balloon itself collapsed, spreading out over the swell. Soon they were covered in the heavy wet material.

Steve checked that Buster's box was still in position.
He swam out a little, holding his head as high as he
could to keep Buster's box clear of the water.

He was immediately aware of a tugging current and
swam back fast . He clung to the basket which was
now heaving about at a forty-five degree angle.

But neither twin replied.

CHAPTER SIX

Raw panic swept through him, but suddenly Steve saw Will struggling, his eyes glazed, weak and unable to get back to the basket. Steve swam towards him slowly, trying to keep his head up to protect Buster. Should he dump him, he wondered. Wasn't human life more valuable than a rat's? He had to save Will.

As he hesitated an enormous wave broke over him and the box floated free.

Steve heard Buster squeak inside the box and a surge of grief came over him. Then Will came splashing towards him, in a frantic dog-paddle, heading for the basket.

You can't do that!

Will had to yell above the howling of the wind.

Can't do what?

Let Buster drown. Save him!

Steve grabbed Buster's box again as Will dog-paddled past him with surprising strength, clutched at the basket, and hung on.

Give me Buster. I'll keep him safe while you find Joe.

Steve could hear Buster squeaking indignantly inside his box. 'Thanks,' he gasped as he handed his precious pet over. 'Joe!' he yelled, swallowing water. 'Where are you, Joe?'

Eventually Steve found Joe floating on his back under the folds of the balloon.

Steve got him in a life-saving position, but Joe was so heavy in his saturated jacket and jeans that Steve could only just keep his head clear of the waves. Joe's eyes were closed and he didn't speak.

Had he already drowned?

Suddenly, to Steve's relief, Joe began to choke, spewing out water and gasping for air. But the heavy folds of wet balloon were pressing down on them both.

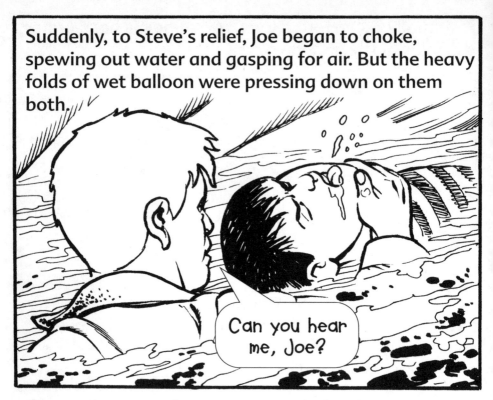

There was no reply. Steve struggled to keep Joe's head above the waves, but gradually he realised he had a hopeless task.

Joe muttered something, but Steve couldn't make out what he was saying. Then he spluttered.

We've got to swim clear of the balloon. If we don't you're going to get even more tangled up.

I can't.

I'm going to let you go and you've got to follow me. Just dog-paddle. It isn't far.

Joe splashed weakly.

51

CHAPTER SEVEN

Steve grabbed the basket and looked back, but there was no sign of Joe.

But then Joe appeared, gasping and spluttering, but just managing to grab the basket.

But it was Steve himself who felt like letting go. He had never been so exhausted. All he wanted to do was give up, close his eyes and slide down into the waves which now felt strangely warm and inviting.

Then, just as Steve began to lose his grip on the basket, he heard an angry squeaking. Will looked down at the box.

Buster doesn't sound very happy.

Steve felt a surge of energy and held out a hand.

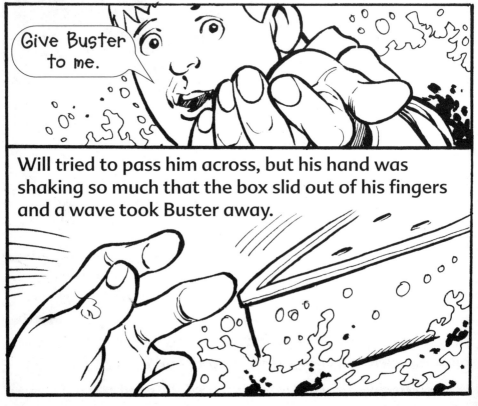

Give Buster to me.

Will tried to pass him across, but his hand was shaking so much that the box slid out of his fingers and a wave took Buster away.

Steve launched himself after Buster in a fast crawl.
He didn't feel in the least tired now.

Dimly he was aware of Will shouting, 'The lifeboat's
coming!' but Steve had to save Buster.

Out of the corner of his eye Steve saw the yellow lifeboat riding high on a wave.

Someone else was shouting at him now, but Steve didn't want to hear. All he could think about was rescuing Buster. He was sure he could hear him squeaking above the roaring of the waves.

Steve saw the box bobbing up and down. Somehow he was just able to grab it before Buster was swept away by the next wave.

'Got you!' Steve yelled in triumph, and holding the box in the air he began to swim his way back towards the lifeboat that was rescuing Will and Joe.

But now his exhaustion had returned and Steve couldn't keep going any longer. Although he still held Buster's box above his head, he was beginning to slow up.

Suddenly the back of his jacket was grabbed and Steve saw a member of the crew leaning out of the lifeboat.

But Steve was too weak and anyway he was still holding Buster's box in the air.

The crewman muttered something and then shouted.

Hand me Buster. I'll make sure he's safe. Then grab the bottom of the ladder.

Using the last of his strength, Steve passed Buster to his rescuer. The man then came halfway down the ladder and grabbed Steve.

The lifeboat hurtled through the waves. A fishing boat was already heading past them, about to recover the balloon.

Steve opened Buster's box to find that someone had given him a piece of cheese which he was nibbling greedily.